KILLER QUILL

Steve Delmar

AuthorHouse™ UK
1663 Liberty Drive
Bloomington, IN 47403 USA
www.authorhouse.co.uk
Phone: 0800 047 8203 (Domestic TFN)
+44 1908 723714 (International)

Published by AuthorHouse 06/21/2019

ISBN: 978-1-7283-8979-0 (sc)
ISBN: 978-1-7283-8978-3 (e)

Print information available on the last page.

authorHOUSE®

All drawings based on original ideas of author. Deep thanks and mighty admiration for illustrators Bill Hope, Bob Stokes and Dave Press.

Front cover *Dave Press*

The bookworm *Bob Stokes*

A chip off some blockheads *Bill Hope*

A cloud's complaint *Bob Stokes*

The future's in parts *Dave Press*

Apart from birth *Bob Stokes*

The natural *Bill Hope*

Dancer *Bob Stokes*

Three flakes *Bill Hope*

Easy money *Bob Stokes*

Love unplugged *Bill Hope*

My little vice *Bob Stokes*

Killer quill *Dave Press*

Star brain *Bob Stokes*

The joy of boyhood *Dave Press/Bill Hope*

Love conquers blister *Bob Stokes*

The innocent bee *Bill Hope*

Act of desperation *Dave Press*

Believe

From the essence that is you
Will evolve a higher truth

Wave your spirit wand
Have whatever you want

The universe is only as it seems
Believe the power of your dreams

A SALAD A DAY
KEEPS THE BUGS AWAY
ALWAYS RINSE THOROUGHLY
AND REMOVE ANY WORMS
OIL
S
P

The bookworm

I’m hooked on cook books
Can’t put ‘em down
Not cos I read ‘em
I’ve just got to eat ‘em!

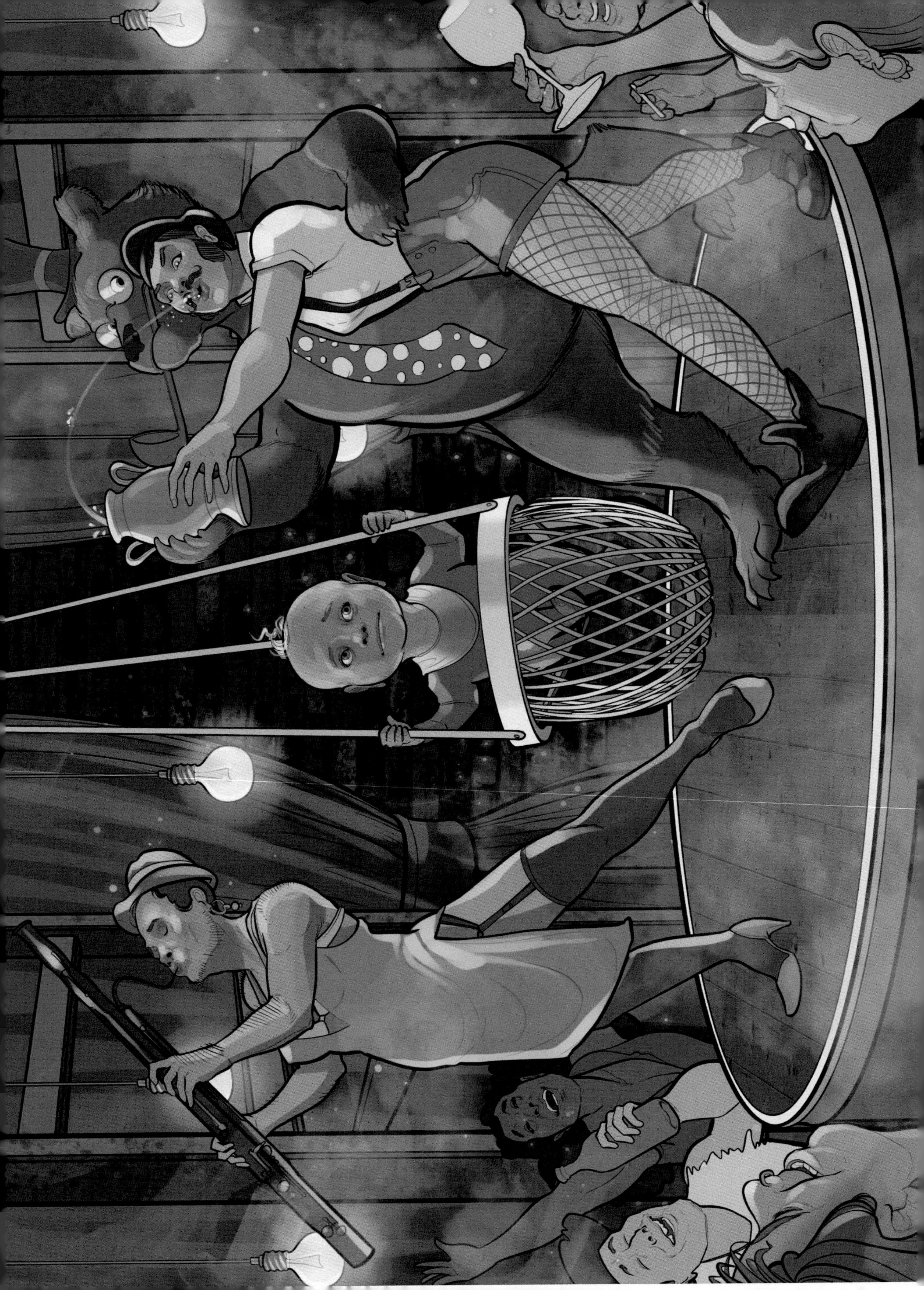

A chip off some blockheads

After the boom and then the zoom
I find myself in a gooey tomb
It's all a bit doom and gloom
There's not much room in a womb

Night after night you make me fume
Insisting on crooning out of tune
Blowing a bassoon, filling a spittoon
And what buffoon sucks a spoon?

I beg for mercy but you always resume!

After nine months in a soupy typhoon
I'm not exactly over the moon
I feel myself about to swoon
And not a moment too soon
I emerge like a star from my cocoon
To a roar of 'encore' from a packed saloon

'So you two goons are my parents, I presume!'

'. . .'

'Who are you calling a prune!'

A cloud's complaint

PLEA TO PILOTS

If you lot don't think we clouds can feel pain
How'd you like *your* guts ripped out by a plane!

All parts
Internal
External
Human
Animal
hybrid

The future's in parts

'Ed, nothing personal, but how about a new head?'
'Oh, there's Blair, scrubbing his plastic hair.'
'Sly, what a guy! The girls just can't resist his square eye.'
'Well, Andy Speers, no more deafness with seven ears.'
'Rose, you pose. Stretching your nose into a hose.'
'Caw! Mr Sproat, love the see-thru throat.'
'Jim, your chin looks so much better with a fin.'
'So, Sidney, after what happened, do you still
recommend a rubber kidney?'
'Ah, Dr Green, it's Jean, how do you oil a spleen?'
'Lover boy Bart, let me guess. You've melted your thirty-third heart.'
'Listen, Cy, this time don't buy a glass thigh, ok?'
'He he, Dee, what a great spot for a knee!'
'Hello Mr Clegg, ever thought about a second leg?'
'I say, Grace, you were right to get a new face.'

Apart from birth

We had a nasty turn, the wife and me
We turn to Family Tree on Channel Three
And there's a pair the image of she and me

The natural

First time on a piano at the age of eight
Hands on the keys with a natural weight
Fingers and thumbs striking gold
A musical state taking hold

I felt like I'd played the piano before
And couldn't wait to compose a score
My pennies all went to the music store
Hours in my bedroom open-jawed

As jazz piano greats spewed notes galore
Whose power to swing left me in awe
Whose style and verve I came to adore
Every solo inspiring me more

Now dad wanted me to take up law
And chose to ignore my musical core
Whereupon began a silent war
Where being a dad became a chore

To a son obsessed with musical lore
From whom melody began to pour
Harmonies fighting tooth and claw
In secret practice behind locked door

As much as I loved him I made my decision
To follow my ambition and be a musician
I became hell-bent without repent
On giving vent to my musical bent

Which I did and never made a cent!

NO
DANCING

Dancer

It’s hard at home - no room for you to groove in
You need more space to try out your routines in
You leave a note saying ‘the bird has flown’
You run away to make it on your own

You chase your dream, you hit the street
You take the risk, you feel the heat
You work those feet to make ends meet
It’s not all cream but it tastes so sweet

You don’t care you’ve got no place to live
Dancing for cash or anything they’ll give
Sleeping rough you have to believe
You know what you want to achieve

You want a crowd to give you their affection
Pleasing fans who make you their selection
For them to see who you really are
Born to dance – One day a star

Three flakes

Lounging in their cloudy bed in the boardroom of creation
The chief executive at the head addresses his delegation

'Now, according to my secretary, Analeez
Today's agenda is creepy crawlies
Tex, let's have some nasty stinging insects, alright?
Blake, make a snake that makes 'em quake, got it?
Ryder, have another go at a spider…try eight legs not five, ok?'

Their hologram heads nod in glee at their jobs
Thank you, God, for empowering these slobs

Three flakes who were just itching to give us the shakes!

CREDIT CARD
1234 5678 9876
I.M.SPENT
EXPIRED
VISA

Easy money

I'm a shopaholic's addiction, a fiscal affliction
A fake financial prop
A modern day scourge for those with the urge
To spend and spend without stop
An all-consuming habit to turn credit into debit
As I'm pushed well over the top
In less than a minute I'm stretched to the limit
Squeezed for every last drop
When I'm all maxed out with no more clout
I'm called a monetary flop
If I remain unpaid, I'm severed with a blade
Watch my credit go pop
Pauper hubby's glad, spender wifey's sad
No more shop till we drop
A heartless end for a flexible friend
Isn't life hard for a credit card!

OLIVES

Love unplugged

SCENE - Cocktail bar

POWER SUPPLY

Hi cutie, how about I turn you on with some vintage voltage?

LIGHT BULB

Excuse me grandpa but I need young current to turn me on.

POWER SUPPLY

But baby, I'm all charged up and raring to flow.

LIGHT BULB

What's a burnt-out power supply like you got to show?

POWER SUPPLY

Hey, I may have an old coil but I've still got the amperage.

LIGHT BULB

From what I can see, you're pumping well below average.

POWER SUPPLY

Don't you worry, honey, I can still turn on the juice.

LIGHT BULB

Get real. Your wires are loose and you've blown a fuse.

POWER SUPPLY

Sugar, you're talking to the King of Essential Potential.

LIGHT BULB

Sweetie, that's your trouble, all urge and no surge.

POWER SUPPLY

It ain't quantity, baby, it's quality, with pedigree circuitry.

LIGHT BULB

Ha! Your vanity's flatter than a dead car battery.

POWER SUPPLY

You know something, light of my life?

LIGHT BULB

Shock me.

POWER SUPPLY

You really know how to turn a power supply OFF!

My little vice

Dear Dr Rumbumjumbo

I took your advice

I screamed 'bile discharge' twice
Boiled up a pan of brown maggot rice
Added one cup of rat-bowel lice
Then a dash of skunk-spray spice

Though it cooked in a trice
And tasted really nice
I'm afraid it didn't cure my vice

I still fancy mice!
Any other ideas?

Yours sincerely

Thomas Katz

INK

Killer quill

God! How he sends me into a rage
Scratching angrily at the page
Digging furrows with my point
Pulling my spine out of joint

Mind you, we wrote some great stuff
Private eye McDuff, he was tough
Until agent Zarf throttled him with his scarf
Wow! That was an action-packed paragraph

After all that zest I should have guessed
He doesn't have a clue what comes next
Here we go; he's sitting back, taking stock
That vacant gape - he's got writer's block

Now I'm in for some royal abuse
He bends me, he chews me
Now I'm a spoon stirring his tea
He throws me like a dart to kill a bee

He kicks off his brogues
Makes me jab his itchy toes
And to add to my woes
Now I'm poking his nose

Without a care he chucks me in the air
Twirls me in his greasy hair
Scrapes me against the leg of his chair
Then my worst fear; I de-wax his ear

Now we're down to low-class farce
He forces me to scratch his arse
Then slams me into his desk top clock
Yelling 'Please God un-lock my writing cock.'

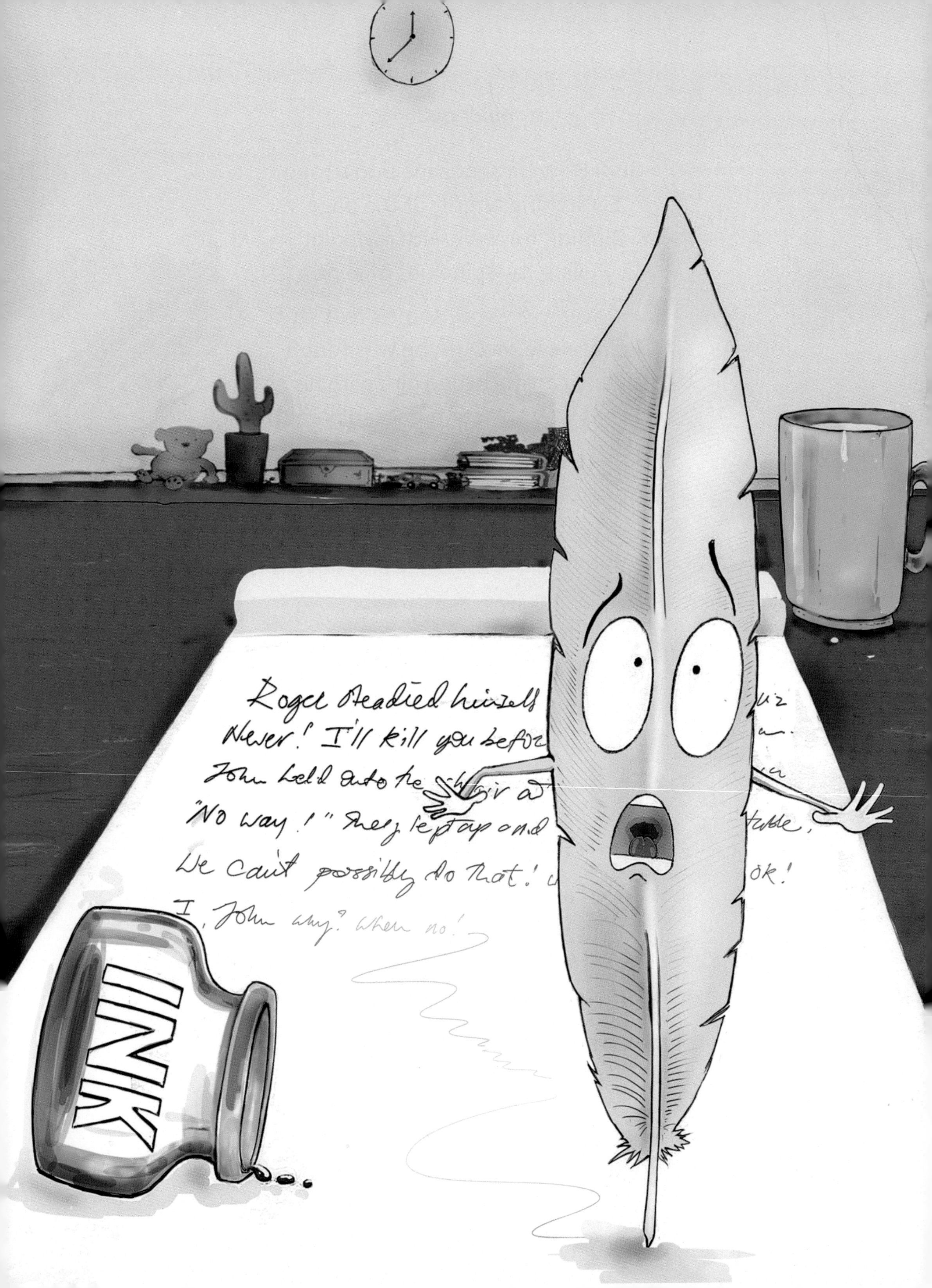
Never! I'll kill you
"No way!"
We can't possibly do that!
INK

But hey! Hold on!
A gleeful grin as I tap his chin
His eyes are wide and sparkling bright
He inks my nib - we begin to write

By Jove! I think he's got it

Slowly at first as the train sets off
But gathering pace as steam blows off
The villain pounces, the damsel cries
In the nick of time the hero arrives

Oh, it's one hell of a fight!

But oh no, what's this? I'm feeling weak
I'm having a dizzy streak
Blast! I'm running out of ink
Keep writing! Don't sever the link!

Does the villain get killed?
Is the hero's blood spilled?
Does he marry Jill?
Was she on the pill?
Oh hell! I feel really ill,
Come on Bill,

HURRY UP WITH THAT REFILL!

Star Brain

The name's Tony Crane, errand boy for movie star Daisy Jane.

She's on location in Spain. Now I don't wanna complain but what a harebrain. I gets a call from the crazy dame.

She whines:

'I'm missing Little Coltrane. Bring him over on the next plane.'

Hah! Little Coltrane happens to be a Great Dane but I need the dough so I play her stupid game. We race to the airport on the the express train but they won't let me put the Dane on the plane. There's another new rabies strain. Guess what? We're back in quarantine . . . AGAIN! I calls up Daisy Jane to explain.

She complains:

'Crane, you're nothing but a pain. If you had half a brain, you'd have made it plain, there ain't no Dane as tame as Little Coltrane.'

I says:

'Jane, why should I take the blame? You're insane. Lay off the cocaine.'

Jane says:

'Crane, you're going down the drain. You're back in the slow lane. Kiss goodbye to the gravy train.'

I says:

'Jane, I should never have introduced you to fame. I liked you much better when you were ON THE GAME!'

Love conquers blister

The ever-expanding Aster Bannister is laid up with a throaty twister. Though her singing style isn't everyone's cup of tea, Aster always gives it her all. But the strain of belting out ear-splitting, window-shattering arias has caused her vocal cords to resonate uncontrollably from the bowels of deep bass to the high peaks of sopranissimo.

A soft yet commanding voice echoes through her conveniently open back door.

'Yoohoo, Miss Bannister, are you up to receiving your adoring music director?'

Aster croaks, swigs some cough medicine, gargles and spits into a bucket by her bed.

'I'm in bed, come up, Mister Lister.'

In a flash, the skinny eager beaver is up and sat beside her.

'Ah, Miss Bannister, how I miss conducting my favourite vocalista.'

Aster blushes, flashes her eyelids and squawks.

'Ooh, is there anything you can do for me, Mister Lister?'

'You betcha. Now open up, I need to insert my finger.'

He does. Aster chokes and splutters.

'Er! Goo you gink I'll egger ging ageng, Gigger Gicker?'

'Don't worry, my dear, it's nothing sinister. No wonder you're struggling to hit the right register. On the back of your throat is a pink bubbly blister.'

Now Aster Bannister is a seductive buxom spinster and Mister Lister can't resist her. He knew just what to administer. He took three tots from his whisky canister and the blister burst when he French kissed her.

512
520

The joy of boyhood

CLEANING TIME
See this? it's a vacuum
"..."
No you're not ill! Clean your room
"...?"
Because it's covered in dust
"..."
Well who said life was just!

BATHTIME
You stink! Get in that bath
"..."
No I'm not having a laugh
And don't miss your face, it's an utter disgrace
And by the way, I know you didn't brush your teeth today
"..."
What do you mean you like the taste of decay?

GETTING DRESSED TIME
God, look at the state of your hair!
"..."
Well you damn well ought to care
Now dress up warm or you'll catch your death
"..."
Did you just swear under your breath?
"..."
Hey, don't lie. Now straighten your tie
"..."
No, you won't die
"..."
And don't mutter, you'll end up with a stutter
Here's a rag, wipe the mud off your shoes
And you can wipe off that look of the falsely accused

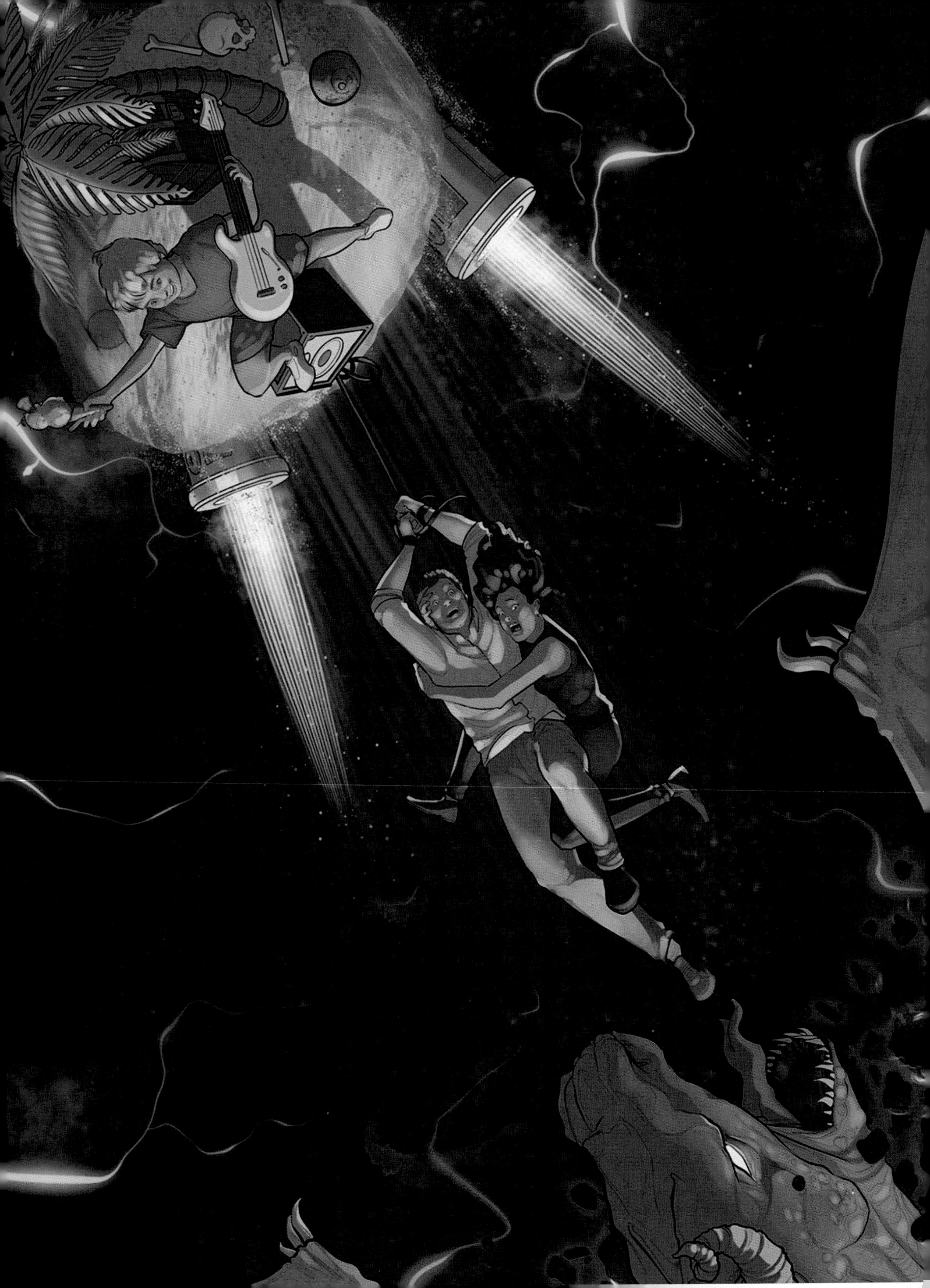

MEALTIME

Hey! Stop kicking your sister under the table

"..."

She did *not* try to strangle you with a cable

Don't you dare flick that meatball with the ladle

DOWNTIME

I've told you before, don't slouch

And please take your feet off the couch

"..."

How dare you! I'm not being a grouch

BEDTIME

Now be polite and kiss grandma goodnight

"..."

Well, try with all your might

"..."

I don't care if she smells funny

Be nice to her and we'll get her money

WISHFUL THINKING TIME

"..."

No you can't go away on a five year cruise

"..."

Hey, when did you learn to sing the Blues?

FACTS OF LIFE TIME

"..."

Well, I'm sorry, but it's for your own good

"..."

Hey, there's worse off than you in the neighbourhood

"..."

Well you're not eighteen, you're only seven

So just do as all boys should . . .

"...?"

Grit your teeth and enjoy your boyhood!

The Innocent bee

My name is Jeremy and I'm a bee. I live in Galaxy Minus Three.

It was a lovely day. I was buzzing around fancy free. I see Henry the flea guzzling honey while basking on the old beech tree. Then out of the blue, my cousin Anthony, from the criminal side of the family, swoops down in glee on a honey stealing spree.

Well! Word of the crime gets around and since I'm a bee I go to ground. A reward is offered by an anonymous vole and I get stitched up by Snitch the mole.

In a pre-dawn raid by the Mantis brigade I'm hauled downtown for an ID parade. Short-sighted Henry points to me! What a nerve! He can't ruddy see.

I can't take prison and I tell 'em so but they'll only listen if I give 'em some dough. But I'm flat broke, it's no joke. We bees are poor folk.

In court I'm struck dumb. The Judge is Henry's mum. I defend myself to a tee. I make my case for mistaken identity but the Queen Flea rejects my plea. She accuses me of perjury and finds me guilty for relieving her Henry of his afternoon tea.

I yell: 'This is a flea conspiracy against the bee minority.'

To which she barks: 'Lock him up and throw away the key.'

My plea for clemency falls on deaf ears. I'm put in solitary for three dead years. So there I lie, severed from my family tree, a falsely accused, wrongly convicted bee.

I pace that cage days and nights raging at the breach of my stinging insect rights. Then God in his mercy hears my prayers. The cell door opens. I'm led upstairs. Justice prevailed. I'm no longer jailed. As I fly into the sun so happy to be free, dragged in in chains is cousin Anthony.

HORSE GUA
RUSSIAN
VODKA

ACT OF DESPERATION

Jack caught the acting bug when he was 10. His vengeful headmaster sentenced him to play Othello in the end-of-term play as a punishment for vomiting carrot mush down the leg of the visiting Mayoress when presented to her as the perfect pupil. His performance was a zinger. The entire school split its sides with raucous laughter. But it was an odd thing. Despite the ridicule, Jack felt at home on the stage; as if he belonged there.

*

After failing all six hundred and twenty-two Othello auditions over the next twenty-seven years, Jack tries a new approach. He auditions for the BBC's flagship soap, *Granny's Abattoir.*

His enthusiastic debut is manna from heaven for the gluttonous press. According to *The Times,* his erotic advances to a slaughtered bull cause parliamentary outrage and put the BBC's license fee at risk. Jack becomes the tabloid's whipping boy. The BBC succumbs to media pressure and kills off his boisterous slaughterhouse floor cleaner character after his first appearance.

*

Jack hits the bottle, then the street.

*

Through a haze of intoxicated amnesia, Jack squints at the salivating press packed into the gallery. The generously bosomed matronly magistrate, Dame Winifred Bliss, clears her throat with an audible warble and adjusts her broad rump. Mr Humper, the lanky, toffee-nosed Crown Counsel, settles his beady eyes on his showbiz-*this is going to be great for my career*-victim swaying in the witness box.

The court hushes. Mr Humper addresses Jack.

'Despite the overwhelming weight of evidence against you, do you still deny committing an act of gross indecency in the Chelsea penthouse bedroom of lingerie model Dawn Prawnthorn M.B.E. between the hours of 10 pm and midnight on New Year's Eve?'

Jack's face is a blend of ingrained hangover and childish innocence. He has absolutely no idea what the man is talking about. If only he could come up with an alibi, but he doesn't have a clue where he was on New Year's Eve.

'Gross indecency?' mutters Jack scratching his crew cut head.

'That's right, Mr Daniels, and I might add that Miss Prawnthorn is dating a respected member of the Royal family.'

The words *'Royal family'* cause a collective intake of breath from Fleet Street's finest scum. Jack's roly-poly barrister, Mr Fawcett, struggles to his feet and splutters his disgust.

'Madam, I object to this insinuation. Crown Counsel should damn well know better than to introduce uncorroborated irrelevant claptrap.'

'Thank you, Mr Fawcett. Now Mr Humper, the existence or otherwise of a relationship between Dawn Prawnthorn and a member of the Royal family has no bearing on the case before the court. Please confine yourself to known facts and leave the lurid imagination stuff to Fleet Street.'

There is an outbreak of accusative finger pointing in the gallery. Mr Humper is unmoved. 'Well, Mr Daniels?'

Jack strains to recall anything of that evidently colourful night. The only thing that comes to mind is a double measure of ultra smooth Scotch whiskey caressing his parched vocal cords. His thirsty jaw falls open and out tumbles a vocal idiocy.

'Did this Prawnthorn chick get the MBE for wearing French knickers?'

Jack's naive stupidity hits everyone's funny bone. The headlinehungry whores squeal with delight. Dame Bliss blushes and raps her block to restore order.

'Come now, Mr Daniels, you're not on television now.'

'Oh thanks, kick a man when he's down, why not?' Jack wipes away a crocodile tear.

Dame Bliss gives him a fake sympathetic nod then points to Mr Humper who presses home his advantage.

‘Mr Daniels, your feeble attempts at acting brought shame upon yourself and the BBC. Do you suppose they will fare better here?’

Jack titters. ‘Well it works for you!’

The press hounds chuckle like fools. Dame Bliss silences them with a glare.

Mr Humper continues: ‘Isn’t it time you faced up to what you really are?’

How can Jack possibly deal with a profound psychological question that goes to the very core of his existence when he has total amnesia on New Year’s Eve?

Mr Fawcett heaves himself up. He dabs his sweating temple with a hanky. ‘Madam, I really must object to Crown Counsel’s relentless onslaught on my client’s character.’

Dame Bliss emits an exasperated huff. ‘Come now, Mr Humper, you know better than to employ character assassination. You’re a lawyer not a journalist.’

The reputation destroyers in the gallery smile with angelic purity.

Mr Humper soldiers on. ‘Well, Mr Daniels, I will ask you again. Do you still deny the charges of lewd conduct?’

Jack doesn’t hear the question. Who are all these people? What is he doing here? How has his life led him to this point? Is he really on trial for a bunch of excessive schoolboy pranks? Or is he on trial for a higher purpose? The answer arrives in a blinding light of revelation. *This isn’t a trial. It’s an audition.*

‘I want to confess something.’

‘Aha!’ declares Mr Humper, ‘I always get my man.’

Jack pounces on the unintended double entendre. ’To do what?’

The press let out an almighty guffaw. Dame Bliss allows herself a tight-lipped smile.

Mr Humper rustles his papers. ‘Yes yes, now let’s stick to the point, shall we?’

Jack winks and puts his hand down the front of his jeans.

Mr Humper explodes. 'What on earth are you doing?'

'I found a point I can stick to.'

The hacks roar. Dame Bliss blushes, hiccups then hammers her block. Mr Humper looks like a guest who has turned up at the wrong party. 'Your Worship, for god's sake, the defendant is committing lewd conduct in open court.'

The guttersnipe news dogs giggle like school kids. The experienced Dame Bliss watches and waits. Her ominous silence settles the court. She addresses Jack.

'Mr Daniels. Are you trying to be funny, or is it a natural ability?'

Cynical remark or not, it sideswipes Jack. Something stirs inside him. He gropes for an answer.

'Well, I, er, I don't know, I never really er, I mean come to think about it I suppose I...'

'That's fine Mr Daniels, I wasn't expecting an answer.'

'Oh I see.'

'Mr Humper, proceed.'

'Yes, Your Worship. Now then, Mr Daniels, what about this confession?'

'Oh yeh. I confess I haven't changed my mind about lawyers.'

The press bite their tongues and gurgle. Dame Bliss smiles. Mr Fawcett coughs. Mr Humper fights back with a blistering salvo.

'Now look here, the long-serving Police Constable Bullock has testified that on the night in question he was sent to a Chelsea apartment in response to a desperate 999 call. On entering said premises a distraught, negligee'd Miss Prawnthorn invited him into her bedroom where he observed you swinging naked from her chandelier whilst French kissing an inflatable Japanese Love Doll. Do you dare contest the evidence of a loyal constable?'

'You forgot about the banana.'

What a punchline!

The courtroom is awash with wild hooting. Jack has them in the palm of his hand and isn't letting go. Neither is Mr Humper.

'Mr Daniels, you are depraved.'

'Well, I do me best.'

Oh, this is too much. Everyone cracks up again. There is no stopping Jack now. Mr Humper's equilibrium is decomposing rapidly.

'This is a court of law, not a circus.'

'Not from where I'm standing, mate.'

Another classic!

Mr Humper's cheeks pulsate with glowing scarlet veins.

'And do you still deny attempting to tango with the hind leg of a Royal Horse Guard's black mare while wearing nothing but a polka dot bikini, one black stiletto and a turban?'

'I did think she was a bit stiff.'

Everyone a winner!

Reporters fall off their seats clutching their guts and groaning with the pain of excessive laughter. Dame Bliss's bun has loosened and she appears to be biting her left index finger. Mr Humper lets protocol go to the dogs and thumps his bench.

'Mr Daniels, you are a traitor to your Queen and country. In earlier times the Tower of London would be your next stop. How can you stoop so low?'

'Easy. I'm used to bending over.'

'Please, no more punch lines,' beg the press. They are in stitches and gasping for air.

Mr Humper abandons any remaining sobriety. He swipes his papers to the floor and slumps onto his bench followed by his toupee.

'Your Worship, the Crown rests its case.'

*

At this point everyone needs a rest. The exhausted hacks crawl back to their seats taking lungfuls of needed air. The sly old dog Mr Fawcett seizes the moment. He forces his imposing weighty frame onto its overwhelmed feet.

‘Your Worship, my client may be a drunken second-rate sacked soap actor but he clearly doesn’t have an ounce of criminal intent in him. I plead no case to answer.’

Jack grins and shrugs his shoulders as if to say *what the hell, I gave it my best shot.* Dame Bliss readjusts her bun, closes her eyes and inhales as if she is sucking air from the Earth’s core. The eyes of the court follow her expanding majestic British Empire chest. After seventeen agonizing seconds she deflates her frontage, pops open her eyes and breaks into a joyous smile.

‘Case dismissed.’

The cheers blow the roof off the court. The press scramble over each other and mob Jack in the witness box. They snap him from every angle, demand autographs, bombard him with technical questions on comic delivery and offer him princely sums for the exclusive rights to his life story. Jack pinches his arm as hard as can. He isn’t dreaming. It’s bleeding.

Printed in the United States
By Bookmasters